MOONBEAR'S DREAM

A MOONBEAR Book

■ FRANK ASCH ■

ALADDIN

NEW YORK   LONDON   TORONTO   SYDNEY   NEW DELHI

ALADDIN

An imprint of Simon & Schuster Children's Publishing Division

1230 Avenue of the Americas, New York, NY 10020

This Aladdin edition August 2014

Copyright © 1999 by Frank Asch

All rights reserved, including the right of reproduction in whole or in part in any form.

ALADDIN is a trademark of Simon & Schuster, Inc., and related logo is a registered trademark of Simon & Schuster, Inc.

For information about special discounts for bulk purchases, please contact Simon & Schuster Special Sales at 1-866-506-1949 or business@simonandschuster.com.

The Simon & Schuster Speakers Bureau can bring authors to your live event. For more information or to book an event contact the Simon & Schuster Speakers Bureau at 1-866-248-3049 or visit our website at www.simonspeakers.com.

Designed by Karina Granda

The text of this book was set in Olympian LT Std.

Manufactured in China 0614 SCP

10 9 8 7 6 5 4 3 2 1

Library of Congress Cataloging-in-Publication Data

Asch, Frank.

Moonbear's dream / Frank Asch.—1st ed.

p. cm.

Summary: When Moonbear and his friend Little Bird see a kangaroo in the backyard, they think they must be dreaming, so they do things they would not do if they were awake.

[1. Bears—Fiction. 2. Birds—Fiction. 3. Dreams—Fiction. 4. Behavior—Fiction.] I. Title.

PZ7.A778Mnk   1999 [E]—dc21   98-24133   CIP AC

ISBN 978-1-4424-9432-9 (pbk)

ISBN 978-1-4424-9433-6 (hc)

ISBN 978-1-4424-9434-3 (eBook)

To Jan

One day a kangaroo with a joey in her pouch escaped from the zoo and wandered through Bear's yard.

"Do you see what I see?" asked Little Bird.

"I sure do," replied Bear. "But I can't believe my eyes. It looks like something from a dream!"

"Maybe we *are* dreaming," chirped Little Bird.

"Yes, that's it!" cried Bear. "We're probably asleep in our beds right now."

"Maybe we should wake ourselves up," said Little Bird.

"Why not have some fun first?" chuckled Bear. He went inside, took down his honey jar, and started scooping out big pawfuls of honey.

"Weren't you saving that honey for winter?" asked Little Bird.

"This is dream honey," said Bear. "I can eat it now and it will still be here when I wake up!"

"What a great idea!" said Little Bird, and he flew to the shelf where he kept his birdseed.

When Bear finished his honey, he dropped the jar on the floor. *Crash!*

"Aren't you going to clean that up?" asked Little Bird.

"Why bother?" said Bear. "When I wake up, the mess will be gone."

"That's right!" chirped Little Bird, and he pushed a vase of flowers off the table. "Let's make a mess!"

"Let's make a *big* mess!" cried Bear.

"What fun!" whooped Little Bird. "And we don't have to clean up! All we have to do is pinch ourselves and wake up. Then everything will be neat and tidy again!"

"I love this dream!" said Bear. "What shall we do next?"

"Let's go for a dream swim and pick some dream berries," chirped Little Bird.

"Okay," agreed Bear, and they walked to the pond.

While the two friends had fun together, the kangaroo wandered into Bear's house.

And that's where the zookeeper found her.

"Oh my!" he cried. "Look what you've done!"

The zookeeper quickly picked up the clutter and swept the floor. He even gave Little Bird new birdseed and fixed Bear's honey jar.

Then he tried to catch his kangaroo.

When Bear and Little Bird returned from the pond, Bear said, "I don't want to see that mess again."

"Me neither!" chirped Little Bird. "Let's wake up!"

"Okay," said Bear, and they pinched themselves.

Then Bear opened his door.

Everything was neat and tidy.

Bear's winter honey jar was full.

And so was Little Bird's seed bag.

"Gosh, that was fun!" said Little Bird. "But how come we're not in our beds?"

Bear thought for a moment.

Then he said, "We must have been sleepwalking."

"All that sleepwalking tired me out." Little Bird yawned.

"Me too." Bear yawned back. "Let's take a nap."

"Sweet dreams," said Bear.
"Sweet dreams," chirped Little Bird.